No Rumbly Pooh's Tumbly

Written by Kelli Kaufmann

Cover illustrated by John Kurtz

Illustrated by the Disney Storybook Artists

Read along as Pooh and his friends go on an expotition to find the rumbly in Pooh's tumbly! You will know it is time to turn the page when you hear this sound.... Are you ready? Let's begin!

One morning Pooh wakes up and feels a bit out of sorts.

"Oh, bother," thinks Pooh to himself. "I feel a little odd. I wonder what the matter is."

Pooh begins to think, think, think. What is this funny feeling he is feeling? Is he sick? No, not even a sniffle. Sad? No, as usual he feels rather sunny. Scared? No, he is safe in his bed. But it is quiet…almost too quiet.

"Oh, well," Pooh thinks to himself. "It is time for my Stoutness Exercises. That will take my mind off things."

"There isn't any doubt that Pooh is rather stout," hums Pooh as he exercises. "Bend to touch your toes, they're farthest from your nose...."

But as Pooh touches his toes and wiggles his nose, he can't help think, think, thinking. Those empty honeypots remind him of something... Honey! And honey makes him think of...Eating! And eating makes Pooh think..."Oh, dear! I'm really not hungry! So that's what's wrong, no rumbly in the tumbly!"

The rumbly in Pooh's tumbly has been a faithful friend and constant companion. Pooh has no idea where the rumbly goes when it goes away because it never went away before!

"I will stay at home today and wait for the rumbly to return," thinks Pooh. "It shouldn't be too long." Pooh waits patiently for a moment. Maybe a Pooh song would help the rumbly find its way back. Pooh tries humming a hum. "When the rumbly comes home, we'll have honey...."

The rumbly doesn't return when Pooh hums a hum. So Pooh decides to go looking for it.

"Maybe the rumbly in my tumbly has gone to see the bees in the trees," thinks Pooh. He remembers once when he and his rumbly looked for honey in this tree. "Hello?" Pooh calls into the tree, not at all sure he wants someone to answer. Happily—or unhappily, depending on how you look at it—no one answers.

Pooh thinks of his good friend Piglet. Perhaps Piglet has seen his rumbly or could help look for it. When Pooh gets to Piglet's house, Piglet is outside sweeping leaves. But it is so windy the leaves are sort of sweeping Piglet.

Pooh tells Piglet about his missing rumbly. "I haven't felt or heard the rumbly in my tumbly all day," says Pooh sadly.

"Oh, dear," says Piglet. "Do we need an expotition? An expotition to find Pooh's rumbly?"

TRESPASSERS
WILL

Pooh and Piglet set off on an expotition to find Pooh's rumbly.
"I hope we find the rumbly soon. Don't you, Piglet?" asks Pooh.
Pooh is afraid that the wind might blow the rumbly away.

"Yes, this is just the sort of wind that could blow away a rumbly,"
Piglet agrees. "If the rumbly were small." Piglet is feeling a bit
windblown himself.

Pooh and Piglet go to Rabbit's house. Pooh thinks his rumbly may have gone to tea with Rabbit. "Rabbit is always so happy to see us," thinks Pooh.

"Hello?" calls Pooh. He is answered by a voice that says, "I'm not home." Pooh asks the voice if it is the rumbly that isn't home, and the voice answers, "It is Rabbit that isn't home."

So Pooh leaves a message with the voice to please tell Rabbit to join Piglet and Pooh on an expotition to find Pooh's rumbly. Finally Pooh finishes leaving the message and Rabbit appears. Happily the expotition continues.

Pooh crawls inside a log to look for his rumbly. Piglet and Rabbit hear strange bounce, bounce, bouncing behind them. Suddenly they think it would be a good idea to join Pooh inside the hollow log!

"Be as quiet as little mice," says Rabbit. Pooh supposes that mice are quiet, so little mice must be very, very quiet.

"Squeak!" says Piglet because he is squished underneath Rabbit. The bouncing gets louder. It's Tigger! Tigger thought he had heard his friends, but it must've been only little mice. So Tigger bounces off, farther into the Hundred-Acre Wood.

After Tigger bounces away, Rabbit sighs with relief. He is in no mood to be bounced by Tigger today. Or any other day either!

"Squeak!" squeaks Piglet again as they push and pull each other out of the log. Pooh and Piglet are tired after all of the excitement. Hunting for a lost rumbly is a big job for a bear of very little brain and a pig of very small size. Pooh sits down to collect his thoughts. Piglet, being a very good friend, sits down to keep Pooh company. Soon they are both sound asleep. Rabbit worries that Tigger might return to bounce him, so Rabbit decides to leave his friends to their nap and head for home.

Pooh and Piglet wake up and continue the expotition. When Christopher Robin hears about the lost rumbly, he says kindly, "Don't worry, silly old bear. Your rumbly will come back. In the meantime, just keep a happy thought."

"I haven't got a happy thought," says Eeyore. "But I have a drum to drum. If you haven't anything better to do." Pooh picks up the drum and thinks about playing a rat-a-tat-tat. Suddenly Pooh has the nicest sort of feeling… He feels hungry! And just like that his rumbly came back!

Everyone is happy to hear that Pooh's rumbly has returned. Except Rabbit, who is afraid that the rumbly will come over for tea. "I found it as soon as I stopped looking," says Pooh happily. "What are ya gonna do to celebrate, Ol' Buddy Bear?" asks Tigger. Pooh thinks for a moment. He really should do something to celebrate. Piglet clears his throat importantly saying, "Oh, excuse me!" and "If you please, everyone!" Piglet asks Pooh and all their friends to please follow him. Piglet has a surprise.